THE WILD WASHERWOMEN

John Yeoman   Quentin Blake

ANDERSEN PRESS

This paperback edition first published in 2009 by Andersen Press Ltd.
First published in Great Britain in 1979 by Hamish Hamilton Ltd.
Published in Australia by Random House Australia Pty.,
Level 3, 100 Pacific Highway, North Sydney, NSW 2060.
Text copyright © John Yeoman, 1979.
Illustration copyright © Quentin Blake, 1979
Printed and bound in Singapore by Tien Wah Press.

10 9 8 7 6 5 4 3 2 1

British Library Cataloguing in Publication Data available.

ISBN 978 1 84270 914 6

This book has been printed on acid-free paper

Once upon a time there were seven washerwomen.

Every day they went down to the river with their baskets of washing on their heads.

Their names were Dottie, Lottie, Molly, Dolly, Winnie, Minnie and Ernestine, and they were all good friends.

When they got to the river they sorted out the clothes and plunged them in. They soaked them. They soaped them. They pounded them on the stones.

They rinsed them. They wrung them. And they spread them over bushes and rocks to dry.

They were the best washerwomen for miles, but they were not happy.
The owner of the laundry, Mr Balthazar Tight, was a very mean
little man, and kept them working from morning to night.

Every morning at the crack of dawn they had to get up and do the ironing before the day's washing arrived. And when it did arrive in the goat-cart, Perkin, the delivery boy, would say, "I'm sorry, ladies, but it's more than ever today."

One morning, as the washerwomen stared glumly at the mountain of dirty laundry, they felt that it was really too much. They all sighed as they looked at the

filthy sheets,

grubby hankies,

horrid socks,

grimy nightshirts,

messy tablecloths

and ghastly towels.

"Why don't we just leave it?"
suggested Ernestine timidly.

Their faces brightened up immediately.

"What a marvellous idea," chuckled Dolly, flinging a grimy shirt across the room.

"Why didn't we think of it before?" chortled Winnie.

And at that they began to dance.

The door burst open and Mr Balthazar Tight stepped in, with Perkin.

"Now, now, ladies," he said with a frown. "There's work to be done."

Then he looked at the great mound of laundry on the floor.
"Wonderful," he said, "there's more than ever."
This made Minnie so angry that she shouted, "Let him have it, girls!"

And the seven washerwomen pushed the mountain of laundry until it collapsed on top of Mr Balthazar Tight. While he was struggling to get free, the seven washerwomen raced out of the laundry and into the yard.

They piled into the empty goat-cart
and Dottie grabbed the reins.
"Gee up, Lysander," she cried
to the goat.

The washerwomen were so excited by their escape that they drove the cart right through the town pond, splashing the clean clothes of the passers-by with muddy water.

After that there was no stopping them. They rode to the market place, where they overturned the stalls and set the animals loose.

They stopped in orchards and climbed the trees to help themselves to the farmers' fruit.

They raced through the hat shops and snatched the hats.

They ran into churches and alarmed the local people by swinging on the bell ropes and making a terrible noise.

The washerwomen were having so much fun that they didn't want it to end. So day after day they went on the rampage. And all that washing had made the washer-women very strong. The people who tried to stop them didn't have a chance.

Everyone was terrified of them. Each village built a watch-tower so that a villager could shout, "Look out, the wild washerwomen are coming!" when their goat-cart came into sight.

In a hut in the forest lived seven woodcutters. They chopped down trees and floated them down the river to the town. When they heard that the seven washerwomen were coming they just laughed. "We'll see who's afraid," they said. "We'll prepare a surprise for them."

The woodcutters decided to make themselves as ugly and as frightening as possible. They tangled their hair and matted their beards. They smeared mud and soot over their hands and faces and clothes. And they practised making blood-curdling cries.

Soon the seven washerwomen came rattling up the mountain path in their goat-cart. As they turned a corner, there in front of them was a terrifying sight. Lysander stopped in his tracks, and even the wild washerwomen were about to run away.

But then Minnie realised that they were looking at the dirtiest and grubbiest things that they had ever seen in their lives.
"Come on, girls," she shouted.
"Remember you're washerwomen!"

They leapt out of the cart and grabbed hold of the woodcutters. They plunged them in the river. They soaked them and squeezed them, and pounded them on the stones. They rinsed them and wrung them and laid them out to dry.

By the time they had finished the woodcutters had never looked so clean and shining, and the washerwomen felt quite proud of their work. In fact, now they could see the woodcutters without their soot and mud, they really rather liked the look of them.

The washerwomen never went back to work for Mr Balthazar Tight. They married the woodcutters, who built them some new log huts to live in. And after that, people who travelled along the mountain path would see them, all happily washing and woodcutting and having the time of their lives.

Also by Quentin Blake